THI
BELONGS TO...

Mr Badger and the Missing Ape

Leigh HOBBS

ALLEN&UNWIN

For Susan Johnson
– my London companion

First published in 2010

Copyright © Leigh Hobbs 2010

Allen & Unwin
83 Alexander Street
Crows Nest NSW 2065 Australia
Phone: (61 2) 8425 0100
Fax: (61 2) 9906 2218
Email: info@allenandunwin.com
Web: www.allenandunwin.com

Cataloguing-in-Publication details are available from the
National Library of Australia www.librariesaustralia.nla.gov.au

ISBN 978 1 74237 418 5

Cover and text design by Sandra Nobes
Set in 15 pt Cochin by Sandra Nobes
Author photograph by Peter Gray
Printed in August 2012 by the SOS Print + Media Group (Aust) Pty Ltd
at 65 Burrows Road Alexandria NSW 2015

5 7 9 10 8 6 4

Contents

CHAPTER 1

Busy Mr Badger

Mr Badger wasn't *just* the Special Events Manager at the Boubles Grand Hotel (pronounced *Boublay*). Because he had been there for so long and knew everyone, as well as just about every*thing* about the hotel, Mr Badger had all sorts of other important responsibilities. And one of the most important was keeping an eye on Algernon.

Algernon stood in the foyer of the hotel. For years, every morning when Mr Badger arrived at work, he would give Algernon a smile. 'How do you do, Algernon!' he would say as he walked past.

Mr Badger knew better than to expect an answer, of course, as Algernon was an ape. A very big ape. And he stood in a glass case.

Algernon had guarded the Boubles Grand Hotel foyer for years and years. Well, not really guarded; he was just there…peering out from his window on the world as if inspecting everyone who arrived at the hotel.

And maybe he was.

Children absolutely adored him, and whether they came to stay in the Boubles Grand Hotel or were just visiting for morning or afternoon tea, saying hello to Algernon was the first thing that every boy and girl wanted to do.

Sometimes there was such a crowd in the foyer that Mr Badger needed to gently organise the children into a queue, so that everyone got to have their own moment or two with Algernon.

Algernon was extremely popular.

Unfortunately, not every child was well behaved.

Sylvia Smothers-Carruthers would often cause trouble. Sometimes even a scene. Just because her grandparents, Sir Cecil and Lady Celia Smothers-Carruthers, owned the Boubles Grand Hotel, she would often try to push into the line.

Or, worse still, when no one was looking, Sylvia would open the glass door of Algernon's case and give him a kick.

'I tell you, Grandma, that thing poked its tongue out at me!' Sylvia would cry.

'Don't be ridiculous,' Lady Celia would snap. 'It's stuffed. I wish your grandfather would throw it out.'

CHAPTER 2

An Alarming
Disappearance

No one, guest or employee, seemed
to remember a time when
Algernon *hadn't* been there in the foyer.

This made Mr Badger's discovery
early one morning all the more
alarming. For when he arrived at the
hotel, walked up the stairs and turned
to say hello to Algernon, he saw that
there *was* no Algernon.

Algernon was…GONE!

Algernon was gone, but where?

At this stage, Miss Pims did not want to ask questions.

It was a dreadful shock. Mr Badger knew that everyone would be upset by Algernon's disappearance. In particular the children. Algernon would have to be found as soon as possible, so Mr Badger began looking straight away.

When his assistant, Miss Pims, arrived at work soon after, she found Mr Badger searching for clues on the floor with a magnifying glass.

'Good morning, Mr Badger,' she said, as if Mr Badger was always on the floor of the foyer peering through his magnifying glass.

'Hello there, Miss Pims,' said Mr Badger. 'I am afraid we have a problem. A serious one. It's Algernon – he's gone!'

Naturally Miss Pims was startled by the news. However, like Mr Badger, she knew better than to panic. She too leapt straight into action.

For a start, she checked Mr Badger's diary. Obviously he would need to be completely free of engagements that day so they could focus on finding Algernon, the missing ape.

CHAPTER 3

The Big Disappointment

By mid-morning a small crowd had gathered in the foyer, and it was a very sorry sight. Disappointed children were arriving and forming a queue, pressing their faces up against Algernon's empty case and fogging up the glass.

Algernon was sorely missed.

Mr Badger and Miss Pims decided that the feelings of the Boubles Grand Hotel's little guests and visitors were of the utmost importance. So, after asking everyone to step back, they covered Algernon's big case with a curtain and hung up a sign that said: 'Algernon is away but will be back shortly.'

Better that the children believe Algernon had gone on holiday, thought Mr Badger, than they be upset by the truth, which was that he'd disappeared.

'That leaves us to do the worrying,'
whispered Mr Badger to Miss Pims.
'I think we should plan our search.'

During morning tea in the dining
room, the most pressing topic of
conversation amongst mothers and
fathers, grandpas, grandmas and
children alike was Algernon: 'Where
do you think Algernon has gone for
his holiday?' and 'When do you
think Algernon will be coming back?'
they said.

CHAPTER 4

A Big Mystery

In their tiny office crammed with bookshelves and filing cabinets, piles of notes, diaries, two desks and chairs, not forgetting all the official Boubles Grand Hotel records, Mr Badger and Miss Pims got to work.

Firstly they listed all the places in the hotel where an ape might fit, or could be hidden.

There were endless possibilities as the Boubles Grand Hotel was big and old, with many guest rooms large and small.

As well, there were staircases, attics, a library, cellars, storerooms, cupboards, bathrooms, four kitchens, the Boubles Grand Hotel Ballroom and two dining rooms.

There were also offices, including the one used by Mr Badger and Miss Pims.

'Well, that's *one* place we don't have to search,' said Miss Pims, looking around. 'We'd certainly have noticed if Algernon was hidden in *here*.'

'Yes, well, where should we start?' said Mr Badger, scratching his furry head. 'I searched the foyer thoroughly this morning, before any of the guests arrived, and didn't find a single clue.'

'How could a big ape just disappear?' asked Miss Pims. 'Who might have carried him away and why?'

'And how could they have lifted him anyway?' said Mr Badger. 'How could they have moved him out of his glass case?'

'So many questions and, as yet, no answers,' sighed Miss Pims.

It certainly was a mystery. One which was *completely* baffling Mr Badger. Miss Pims made two lists: one for herself and one for Mr Badger. Miss Pims was to search the main hotel rooms, and Mr Badger the more out-of-the-way places.

CHAPTER 5

The Search

Miss Pims moved from room to room.

She peered behind curtains in the Boubles Grand Hotel Ballroom, then looked for clues beneath tables and sofas in the dining room where morning tea was being served. She even asked some guests if they wouldn't mind lifting their feet.

24

Miss Pims looked everywhere.

'Just housekeeping,' said Miss Pims, with a smile, every time a guest appeared slightly alarmed as she ticked off her 'rooms inspected' list. Of course, she didn't tell them what she was *really* looking for.

Meanwhile, with his torch and magnifying glass, Mr Badger climbed up stairs, tapped on walls, probed in

dusty storerooms, and opened long-lost doors. He was searching all the hidden, out-of-the-way places he could find.

The Boubles Grand Hotel wasn't just grand ballrooms and marble columns. There were lots of tiny rooms too, easily overlooked and sometimes even boarded up.

The hotel was very large. In fact, there were many parts that Mr Badger hadn't explored for years, parts he had not seen since he was little. At this time, he would follow his father about while he fulfilled his duties as Head Waiter at the Boubles Grand Hotel.

There were rooms full of untouched Boubles Grand Hotel towels and tablecloths, and shelves of ancient Boubles Grand Hotel china jugs and glass vases. Mr Badger found a pantry with abandoned pots and pans from the hotel kitchens and another room full of nothing but broken clocks.

Alas, nowhere was there any sign of... Algernon.

CHAPTER 6

The Secret Room

After hours of searching, Mr Badger came across a door with a handwritten sign saying:

'TOP SECRET...DO NOT ENTER.'

Mr Badger opened the door and crept in.

The walls were covered with framed photographs. He looked carefully, his eyes adjusting to the dim light. At first he thought he was seeing things. These were old photographs, of a very young Sir Cecil Smothers-Carruthers.

Sometimes Mr Badger had to ignore instructions.

In fact, they were *all* of Sir Cecil –
well, Sir Cecil was certainly *in* all of
them. They showed Sir Cecil on safari.
Mr Badger could tell this was so, as not
only was Sir Cecil wearing a pith helmet,
but in one photograph he was sitting on
top of an elephant, and in another he
was chasing butterflies with a net. There
were also quite a few of him peering
through binoculars at wild animals in
the distance.

Resting on a shelf were the very
same binoculars and pith helmet which
appeared in the photographs. Next
to them was a pair of hiking boots and
a rucksack. Mr Badger was amazed,
to say the least.

However, he was about to get an even greater surprise, for on the wall opposite were yet more photographs. And these had another familiar face in them.

Mr Badger moved up close and gasped. Looking back at him was Sir Cecil Smothers-Carruthers, but he wasn't alone. For with him was a slightly smaller, but still instantly recognisable, and even then very big, Algernon.

There they were, sitting in the jungle with a plate of scones and jam between them, sharing a pot of tea and a banana cake. Next to that was a photograph of them shaking hands, laughing and looking at the camera. In another, Algernon was wearing a pith helmet – Sir Cecil's, no doubt.

Mr Badger had always known Sir Cecil was terribly fond of Algernon, even if he was stuffed and standing in a glass case. 'Outrageous!' Sir Cecil would mutter whenever Lady Celia suggested a complete hotel clean-out and major redecoration, starting with the tossing out of Algernon.

'What good is that old ape anyway?'
she would say. 'That flea-bitten beast
in the foyer sends a very poor message
to our guests. It makes them think
that they're staying in a zoo.
As well, it frightens our dear little
granddaughter, Sylvia.'

Sir Cecil would have none of it.
'The ape stays,' he would always say,
'and that is that.'

Now Mr Badger thought he
understood why.

*Sir Cecil refused to budge where
Algernon was concerned.*

CHAPTER SEVEN

A Clue at Last

It was getting late. The dining rooms were closed and the lights had been dimmed. Visitors had left for home, while upstairs the Boubles Grand Hotel guests were tucked into their comfortable beds, undoubtedly enjoying the hotel's speciality – the famous late-night Boubles Grand Hotel hot chocolate.

Back downstairs in their office, however, Miss Pims and Mr Badger were meeting as planned, to discuss the progress of their search.

'I looked everywhere on my list and found nothing,' said Miss Pims, a little downcast.

'I've not found him either,' replied
Mr Badger, choosing his words carefully.
He thought it best to keep the discovery
of the secret room a secret, for the time
being anyway.

Mr Badger was concerned that
Sir Cecil Smothers-Carruthers would
be terribly upset once he knew
Algernon had disappeared. So he
decided he would stay all night and
continue to look for the missing ape.

He suggested to Miss Pims that she
may as well go home.

'No need for us both to go without sleep,' he said with a faint smile. Then he phoned Mrs Badger to explain the situation. Mr Badger didn't want her worrying.

'Yes, my dear, it's a very strange thing, a mysterious disappearance which must be solved as soon as possible. I'll see you tomorrow, and I do indeed have a clean spare uniform.'

He put down the phone and said goodnight to Miss Pims.

'And goodnight to you too, Mr Badger. I'm sure we'll find him, so try not to worry.'

As she left, Miss Pims called back over her shoulder, 'By the way, I noticed the floor of Algernon's case needs repairing.'

CHAPTER 8

A Crack in the Floor

Mr Badger thought he may as well look at Algernon's case straight away.

Once in the foyer, he removed the curtain, opened the glass door and, sure enough, saw a small crack in the wooden floor. It looked easily repairable. Mr Badger was about to turn and leave when he noticed a tiny handle, in a spot usually covered

by Algernon's big left foot. Bending down, so as to inspect it closely, he saw that the handle was attached to a trapdoor.

Carefully, Mr Badger lifted the lid
and shone his torch into the darkness.
Then he bravely climbed down the
steps into a strange part of the Boubles
Grand Hotel. Strange because it was
certainly a part that *he'd* not known
about. At the bottom of the steps,
Mr Badger peered along a corridor
lit by some lamps hanging from the
walls. Near the steps were a few pairs
of very large carpet slippers.

As well, there were footprints on the
floor. They were big footprints, too big
to be human.

Mr Badger studied them with his torch and magnifying glass. They looked like they belonged to an ape. He turned and briskly moved along the passageway, zigzagging beneath the Boubles Grand Hotel, along a path that no guests ever saw.

His torch flashed up and down on the crumbling paint of the walls and ceiling. Suddenly the corridor came to an end in front of two large doors.

46

There was a little light alongside them, and a button. It was the entrance to a lift.

Mr Badger pressed the button and the doors opened.

Inside the lift there was only one button and it said 'Top-floor Flat'.

47

CHAPTER 9

Sir Cecil's Secret

The lift made strange cranking and grinding noises as it lurched its way up.

After a shudder and a jolt, it finally stopped, the doors opened, and Mr Badger stepped out. It was dark. Though not *completely* dark, for beneath a door opposite he could see a thin sliver of light.

Mr Badger crept across to the door, held his breath and silently turned the handle.

Gently, he pushed the door open, just a tiny bit.

Just enough to take a peek inside.

What he saw now was truly a big surprise. With his white gloved paw, Mr Badger stifled a gasp of amazement.

For inside a very comfortable-
looking sitting room with nice furniture
and carpets, tables and lamps, sat two
figures laughing and chatting, enjoying
a cup of tea. In between them, on a
table covered with a fresh white cloth,
was a plate with scones and jam and
cream, what appeared to be the remains
of a big banana cake, a teapot and a
snakes-and-ladders game in progress.
It looked like a tea party. It *was* a tea
party, and it appeared that it had been
going on all day and all night!

A tea party was in progress.

There was Sir Cecil Smothers-Carruthers and, pouring the tea and about to eat a scone, was Algernon.

They were chatting about their times together in the jungle, reminiscing about how Sir Cecil had brought Algernon back to live in the hotel and how funny it was that Algernon had had to learn to 'stand still, *very* still' in his glass box during the day. It wasn't that difficult for him as apparently he had learnt to sleep with his eyes open when he was a baby.

Hiding behind the door, Mr Badger stood and listened for a long time. Gradually he put two and two together and a very strange story emerged.

Incredible as it may seem, it appeared that this was Algernon's home. Apparently, as soon as it was late and everyone was asleep, Algernon would sneak down through the trapdoor, then up to this, his own special flat on the top floor, and watch TV, cook a meal, or just read and relax.

Sometimes he might have Sir Cecil over for dinner and a game or two of snakes and ladders. That's if Algernon was in the mood to cook.

After a while, Mr Badger checked his watch and then looked at the clock on the wall. It was two minutes before five in the morning, but the clock on the wall had stopped. Not only that, Mr Badger noticed that the hour hand had fallen off and was lying on the floor.

Algernon hadn't really disappeared at all. He was just late for work!

For these two old friends, time had stood still.

CHAPTER 10

A Race against Time

M r Badger didn't want the children to be disappointed any longer than necessary by Algernon's absence. There was no time to waste.

While Sir Cecil and Algernon
were deep in conversation, Mr Badger
crept into the room, picked up the hour
hand and carefully hooked it back
into place.

As soon as he was out of the room,
the clock struck five times. The noise
was deafening, fortunately covering
up the creaking sounds of the lift
doors opening.

Just before the doors closed,
Mr Badger heard Sir Cecil say, 'Good
heavens! Look at the time, I must be
going. And so must you, old chap.'

So while Algernon cleared away the
plates, gathered up the photographs
and closed the snakes-and-ladders
board, Sir Cecil put on his jacket and
straightened his bow-tie.

Mr Badger scurried along the
secret passageway, climbed the stairs,
opened the trapdoor and crept out of
Algernon's case into the foyer just in the
nick of time.

59

He heard footsteps coming up
from beneath the floor and quickly
hid behind a marble column. Slowly,
the trapdoor opened. A head and then
a body appeared from the floor of
Algernon's case.

Algernon was back.

Mr Badger always liked to look his best.

It was morning – too late for
Mr Badger to go home. So, in his office,
he put on a clean uniform and made
a note in his diary. There was a clock
on the top floor that needed a regular
check.

But for now there were other things
to think about. Breakfast was soon to
be served.

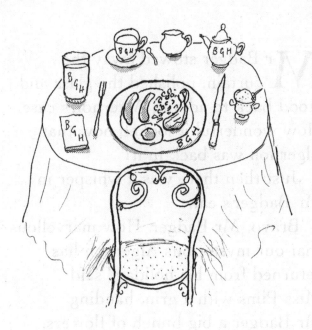

CHAPTER 11

A Welcome Return

M r Badger stowed away the
curtain, polished the glass and
stood back to admire Algernon's case.
How wonderful it looked now that
Algernon was back in it!

Just then there was a whisper in
Mr Badger's ear.

'Bravo, Mr Badger. How marvellous
that our mysterious Algernon has
returned from his holiday,' said
Miss Pims with a grin, handing
Mr Badger a big bunch of flowers.

Later that morning there were
definitely more people in the foyer of
the Boubles Grand Hotel than usual.

This was perfectly understandable, as news of Algernon's return had travelled fast.

And it wasn't just the children who were lined up to see him, eager to ask where he had been for his holiday.

Grown-ups, too – employees and guests – wanted to see for themselves that Algernon was really back. There was such excitement that Mr Badger's crowd-control skills were needed to keep the line orderly.

It wasn't really too much of a surprise, however, that *someone* misbehaved. Sylvia Smothers-Carruthers, arriving for morning tea with her grandmother, pushed into the queue and inspected Algernon, who as usual was standing absolutely still.

Sylvia screwed up her nose and poked her tongue out at the ape in the big glass case.

Quick as a flash, Algernon screwed up his nose and poked out his tongue right back at her.

'That ape poked its tongue out at me!' cried Sylvia, stamping her foot.

'Oh don't be ridiculous,' replied Lady Celia Smothers-Carruthers, dragging Sylvia off into the dining room. 'That thing hasn't moved for fifty years.'

Of course, no one but Mr Badger knew about Sir Cecil's and Algernon's secret.

And even they didn't know that he knew.

Although, strangely, from that day on, when Mr Badger arrived for work in the mornings and greeted Algernon with a hello and a smile – as he had always done – Mr Badger felt sure that he saw Algernon give a little smile back.

And sometimes even a wink.

The End

More Leigh Hobbs books for you
to enjoy from Allen & Unwin

Horrible Harriet
Hooray for Horrible Harriet
4F for Freaks
Freaks Ahoy
Old Tom's Big Book of Beauty
Mr Chicken Goes to Paris
and of course the Mr Badger books

For more details, visit Leigh's website:
www.leighhobbs.com.au

Collect all of Mr Badger's adventures
at the Boubles Grand Hotel.

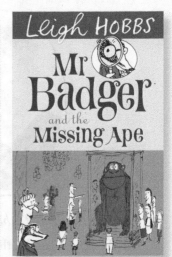

A Little Bit about the Author

Mr Badger is unlike the rest of Leigh Hobbs' characters, as he lives in a real city – London.

Many years ago, Leigh lived there too. Every day he would catch a bright-red double-decker bus into the centre of London, hop off at Trafalgar Square, and set off in a different direction.

Occasionally, Leigh would walk past a place quite similar to the Boubles Grand Hotel. Sometimes he even put on a tie and went in for afternoon tea.

Alas, these must have been the very days when Mr Badger was busy doing other things rather than helping serve tea and scones with jam, for he and Leigh never met…back then.